Chapter 1

Golden Stars and a Yellow Moon

When Rory's Mam brought him home from the hospital he was four days old. She'd painted the big bedroom blue and white to welcome home her new baby boy.

On the blue walls she painted white zig-zag waves like a stormy sea. She drew golden stars on the white ceiling and right in the middle a fat yellow moon. She bought a deep blue cot, with yellow ducks on the sides, for Rory in 'Little Baby Buntings' in Bonnybrook and it was the nicest cot in the whole of the shop.

It was a cold January day when Rory came home and
the garden was covered in soft powdery snow.
The trees on the avenue were bare and spindly and it was
dark by four o'clock. Rory's Mam had the heating on
and she drew the curtains to shut out the grey winter
street. The house was cosy and warm and Rory's Mam
was very happy with her new baby boy.

'Time to make your bottle, pet,' she said, and smiling
down at him she started to sing:

> 'Rory Rashers,
> What a smasher,
> He's my darling little son,
> Diddle dum, diddle, dum dum,
> You and me will have some fun.'

She had a sweet voice. She sang softly and if all the
new babies in all the houses, on all the streets, in all
the towns, in all the countries in all the world had
such a Mam singing such a lovely song they would
have smiled and gurgled and been the happiest babies
that ever were born on a cold January day.

But when she bent down to stroke her little boy's soft
cheek he opened his tiny mouth and he
ROARED AND HE ROARED AND HE ROARED.

'Be patient little fellow,' she said, 'soon your bottle will
be ready.'
But Rory kept on roaring until she brought his bottle.
Every day and every night when Rory wanted to be
fed, or have his nappy changed, or was looking for his
doo-dee, he opened his mouth and he roared.

He roared in the morning, he roared in the afternoon, he roared in the evening and he roared loudest of all at night. Poor Mam's head was sore all the time and she got so little sleep that her little curranty eyes were like black holes sunken into her head.

Sometimes in the night she would cover her sore head with the duvet and cry until morning.

She would cry from the pain in her head. She would cry because Rory's screaming was so loud. She would cry because she was so so tired and she would cry because she was lonely.

When Rory was three and nine months Mam put his name down for playschool.

She'd seen an advertisement in the paper for women with little fingers, pink legs, and small brown eyes to work in a crisp factory just a bus ride away from her house.
She had fat short little fingers, the pinkest of legs, and her eyes were small and brown.

'This job is made for me,' she told herself, 'and now that Rory is starting playschool maybe he'll be taught to stop roaring. I certainly can't manage him. The money will help too and it's time Rory mixed with other children.'

So she took down her best notebook from the top of the wardrobe and with her extra special silver pen she wrote a letter to the manager:

Mr Daniel A. Dandelion
Crisp Factory,
Dublin,
Ireland,
The World, The Universe.

That should cover it, she thought. Then she licked a stamp, popped her letter in a fat brown envelope and stuck it in the letter box just down the road.

In two weeks she got a letter from Mr Dandelion.. She tore the envelope open and read it. It said, in big black letters:

Dear Mrs Rashers,

> *Please present yourself on Thursday*
> *at 3 p.m. sharp for interview.*
> *Late attendance will not be tolerated.*

> *Yours faithfully,*
> *D. Dandelion.*

On the morning of the interview, Mam got her hair done in *Carol's Cut and Curl Up*. She dressed herself in her best blue dress, pushed her little toes into her black strappy shoes, and set off. She left Rory with Mrs Cheese, her next door neighbour.

Mr Dandelion's office was on the top floor of the factory. He was a long, skinny sort of man. He stooped a little at the shoulders and his toes turned up. He was shaped a bit like a banana.

He stood up from his big desk, shook Mam by the hand and told her to sit down.

'Make yourself comfortable, dear lady. I must say I'm loving the hair.'

'Carol in *Carol's Cut and Curl Up* did it,' replied Mam, 'you can always depend on her to do a good job, and she never over charges.'

'That's nice. Anyway, let me give you a short description of our fine business. We like our workers to be part of the company.'

'That's good,' said Mam. She slid her poor sore toes out of her shoes and settled down to listen.

'This is a family business. Cousin Spudsy, a real charmer, is in charge of chopping, cutting and sorting the crips.

Nephew Potato Nose, solid worker, runs the packing department. Little sister Daisy Pinks has a delicate touch. She trains staff how to bake the crisps and I manage the whole operation. We make straight crisps, curly crisps, low salt, high salt and no salt at all crisps.

Mr Dandelion's big face beamed as he continued: 'We also make cheese and onion, salt and vinegar, smokey bacon, low fat, no fat and full to the brim of fat. Our crisps are exported all over the globe. We need extra-special people to make our extra-special crisps.'

He cleared his throat as if something important was coming: 'We like small dainty fingers because they're gentle. Big mashers would destroy the flavour.

Our crisps come from the finest of potatoes, grown on the
farm by my brother, Golden Wonder, and must be
handled with care.

Pink is my favourite colour, as you may observe from my
pink cheeks, my pink bald head, my pink pants and matching
jacket. My dear sister Daisy Pinks has pink legs and brown
eyes, just like yours'.

Mam felt her heart rise as he stood up. 'Mam Rashers,
you fill all our requirements. I can safely say you'll be
just perfect. The job is yours. By the way, do you have
children, may I ask?'

'I have a boy of three and he starts playschool
tomorrow. The hours are ten to half past twelve so this
job is just what the doctor ordered,' replied Mam, 'just
what the doctor ordered.

I can drop Rory into the school, get the bus to the factory and
be home again to collect him at half twelve on the button.'

'Lovely, bubbly,' said Mr Dandelion, 'Start tomorrow at
fourteen minutes past ten then. Blue uniform provided.

Free crisps every second Friday of the month and an extra
bonus bag at Christmas. All staff are invited to a gala dance on
New Year's Eve and you may bring Rory's Dad if you so
wish.'

Thank you, Mr Dandelion,' Mam replied, 'but Rory's dad doesn't live with us. It's just me and Rory.'

'Well, not to worry', replied Mr Dandelion, 'Report for duty next Monday, ten fourteen sharp.'

'Ten fourteen? I'll be there, Mr Dandelion. You've made my day.'

She rushed home to tell Rory the good news but Rory wasn't really interested. He just opened his mouth and ROARED, ROARED AND ROARED.

'Rory Rashers, stop that screaming. We're starting a new adventure tomorrow. You'll make loads of pals at playschool and I've got a job. This is the best news ever.'

'I DON'T WANT TO GO TO PLAYSCHOOL,' he screamed, 'you have to stay here and mind me. That's a mam's job.'

All night long Rory roared. At twenty past four in the morning he was still screeching like a wild animal in the jungle.

The whole house felt his roars. The cups in the cupboard shook and shivered, knives and forks rattled and danced, pots and pans clanked and clattered. In the fridge the eggs smashed themselvs into the milk bottles.

Next door Mr Cheese's false teeth were thrown from his bedside locker and splintered into a hundred pieces. He stamped his foot in anger because he knew it would cost him 300 euro to get a new pair.
Mam climbed out of bed and marched into Rory's room.
'Rory Rashers, for God's sake, stop! You've school in the morning. Will you please just go to sleep. I never heard such a racket.'

'Don't want to go to sleep. I hate you, I WANT MY DAD.'

'You want who?'

'MY DAD. WHERE'S MY DAD?'

It was the first time she ever heard Rory mention his Dad. Her heart turned over.

'Oh Rory, love, come here to me, you poor little fellow.'

Mam lifted him from the bed and sat him on her knee.

'Your Dad's gone away. I don't know where he is, darling.'

'Well I want him,' screamed Rory. Why did he go away? Why doesn't he live with us?'

'Your Dad went away six months before you, my precious little dote, were born.'

'Why? Why did he go?'

'Maybe he was too young to be a Dad. I don't know Rory. That's life.'

'Why was he too young? Was he a little boy? Was he small like me?'

'No, not small. He was big with black hair and eyes like the sea. But he was young, very young.'

'Well he should have stayed and minded us. I hate him.'

'No, Rory, don't hate him, love.' 'I do. I hate him,' said Rory, bucketing tears as he pulled the duvet over him.

Mam went back to her room. She lay awake for a long time listening to the pelting of the rain against the window.

Next morning she dragged Rory from his bed, raced down to the playschool and handed him over to Mrs Tess Toffee, the lady in charge.

'I think he's a bit scared,' said Mam, 'but I'll bet my boots he'll settle in after a few days'.

'Not to worry,' replied Mrs Toffee, 'lots of children cry for

a day or two but very soon they're fine. We've been minding
children for twenty three years and we know how to keep
them happy. Oh yes we do.'

Mam was delighted. She skipped down the road and
climbed onto the bus with her happy little pink legs in tow.

The playschool was one large room with little desks and
lots of toys. There was an easel where you could paint,
blocks to build with, all kinds of costumes to dress up in
and a grassy patch outside with swings, little bikes and
slides.

'It's great fun here,' Jack Toenails told Rory, 'and we get
apple slices and a glass of orange later on.'

'I WANT MY MAM,' screamed Rory, 'I HATE this place.'

He howled until he was hoarse. Mrs Toffee sat him on her
knee and spoke quietly to him.

'There, there,' she whispered, 'you're a big boy now.
Big boys don't cry.'

'Shut up, sticky toffee. I want my Mam.'

When the children sat round for lunch Rory grabbed
Belinda Bun's apple and threw it into her drink. He
turned his chair upside down and kicked Mrs Toffee
on her sore ankle.
'Ouch,' she yelled, 'that ankle is swollen, boy. CALM
DOWN!'

'It's fat,' said Rory, 'like your horrible sticky face.'

'I'm going to have a chat with your Mam,' said Mrs Toffee, ' she will be very disappointed in you.'

At twelve thirty sharp Mam ran up the driveway of the playschool panting and puffing.

'Oh, just in time,' she said, 'what a day. Hope Rory was a good boy, Mrs Toffee.'

'I'm afraid I have some bad new for you. This boy takes the biscuit,' said Mrs Toffee, 'just takes the biscuit. I'm sorry, Mam Rashers but he's upsetting the children, the staff, and the serious lady who does the lunches.

On top of that he kicked me in my poor sore ankle. The child has no manners. Until he learns to stop roaring you'll have to keep him at home.'

'Oh no,' sighed Mam, 'what will I do?' I'll lose my lovely job. Please, please, please and please, give him another chance.'

'Come down to my office and we'll have a chat,' said Mrs Toffee.

She led them to a small room.

'The thing,' said Mam, 'is that I love my new job. We need the money and he WILL pull up his socks. I promise.' Two salty tears rolled down her cheeks as she spoke.

'There, there, no need to get so upset. I don't want you to lose your job.'

Telling them to sit down, she took out a big file from a drawer before she spoke.

'Every other boy and girl in this school does what,they're told,' she said. They don't give backchat toMthe teachers or kick them in the ankles. They don't stand on chairs and destroy good food.'

'Did Rory do all that?' Mam asked, 'all in one day?' Mrs Toffee nodded grimly

'I didn't mean it,' pleaded Rory, 'I just want to stay with you, Mam.'

'I don't know what to do with you,' said Mam sadly, and she put her arm round Rory. She felt sorry for her troubled little boy. What, oh what, was she going to do with him? Maybe if his dad was around things would be different. It wasn't easy being a mam and a dad.
'One more chance, and that's it,' Mrs Toffee warned.

A boy with black spiky hair was coming in the gate as they walked away from the school.

'Will you take a look at his silly hair, Mam,' said Rory 'and his mother is so SKINNY.' He stuck out his tongue at the pair of them and chuckled.

'Come on, Tom,' snapped the boy's mother, 'ignore him. Mrs Toffee won't keep a child like that in her school or she wants her head examined.

You and me have bigger fish to fry. We'll have the last laugh on that ignoramus.'

CHAPTER 2

More Trouble For Rory

The next day the very same thing happened. Mam had a great day at work. Mr Dandelion told her he was very pleased with her and that she'd make a top class crisp maker. As soon as it got to half twelve she arrived at the school.

Mrs Toffee was standing at the gate waiting for her. Clutched to her was Rory, looking like a prisoner.

'Give me the bad news,' whimpered Mam.

Mrs Toffee frogmarched the pair of them to the office again, her big boots clacking on the stone floor. She sat down, took out the file and snorted.

'Your delightful son pulled Chloe's ears today until they were beetroot,' announced Mrs Toffee.

She went on: 'I had to phone Chloe's father. You're lucky he's not here now or World War 3 might break out.

He was breathing fire, saying he'd take Chloe out of the school if this ever happened again.'

Mam looked at Rory. 'Is that true, Rory?' she asked. Rory could hardly remember. Why were they going on about something that didn't matter. It wasn't like the little brat's ears were going to stay red forever. She deserved it anyway, for not letting him do his colouring on her page.

Rory looked round the room. There were pictures of every country in the world on the walls (which bored him) and on Mrs Toffee's table loads of lollipops for what she called 'The Good Boys'.

But there would be no lollipops for Rory.

'If this kind of thing continues,' Mrs Toffee told Mam, putting on that pinched thin-lipped face she liked to use when she meant business, 'we'll have to close down the school, and then where would we be? Wouldn't that be a fine how-do-you-do?'

Rory just put his head down.

'We'll either have to close it down or get rid of you, Mr Rory,' she declared. 'Why should we have children like you here? If everyone gave everyone else beetroot ears, what kind of country would we have?'

'I don't like Chloe, and her dad is a smelly man,' he mumbled. 'I'm glad my dad's not like that.'

'Now, Rory, apologise,' urged Mam, 'I'm sure Chloe's dad is a lovely person.'

'Not as good as mine,' boasted Rory, 'my dad is bigger and stronger.'

Mam took out a tissue and started to sniffle into it. 'I'm sorry, Mam,' Rory whispered, putting his arms round her.

'I'd like to keep him, but it's impossible,' Mrs Toffee concluded. 'Maybe next year he'll have grown up a bit and may be ready for playschool. Try next year Mam Rashers, that's my final word.'

Mam didn't talk to Rory all the way home. She wouldn't let him watch a DVD when they got to the house, keeping the television off. When he went to go out to the back garden she said, 'No, you're grounded.' What did 'grounded' mean, Rory wondered. He felt a prisoner here too, like at the school.

Mam sent him to his room with his tattered old schoolbag. He sat looking at it for hours, then looking out at the sad moon scuttling through the clouds as the evening came down. Would this terrible day ever end?

After a long time he feel asleep so he didn't hear Mam come into his room and cover him with his favourite blue blanket. He didn't see her switch off the light and he didn't hear her crying all through the long night.

Next morning Mam told Rory she had to leave her job. She was going to stay at home with him until he was six and ready for big school.

Every day and every night, week in and week out, she listened to Rory's roars. Her head hurt more and more and she was tired all the time.

The white waves and the golden stars were dirty now and you couldn't even see the yellow moon, but she was too miserable to paint them again.

She was sad because she missed all the other women in the factory, especially her friend Mary Rose. She was sad because her boy was'nt at school like other children.

And she was sad for other secret reasons.

CHAPTER 3

Sean Shares his Sandwiches

Time passed and the seasons changed. Yellow, gold and red leaves curled up on the footpaths of Artane and lay ragged in the gutters. Then winter slyly stolemin. The snow fell and they had a white Christmas.

Rory and Mam snuggled up together away from the cold. Old Mrs Bathtub fell on the ice and broke her leg just outside the chemist's shop on the Tonlegee Road.

In January a cold harsh spring with its grey skies and biting
winds scurried and whistled along through avenues and parks.
A mild summer arrived, warming the toes and noses of the
children as they passed by Rory's door on their way to Mrs
Toffee's school.

Rory stuck out his tongue at them. 'Hope you're
enjoying Mrs Sticky Toffee,' he jeered.

Mam stayed in most days till twelve. Her head ached.
She missed the crisp factory. She was tired all the time.
The wooden floor in the kitchen was streaked with
dirt and the carpet in the living-room had stains of
spilt coca-cola and take-away chips.

Green smelly stuff grew out of a forgotten mug hidden behind
the plastic curtain in the bathroom.

And still Rory roared.

Mr Dandelion left three messages on Mam's mobile.
One in June, one in January and one in March. 'Your
job is here whenever you're ready,' he said, 'just turn
up for duty anytime.'

Days, weeks, months passed by and it was autumn
again. Rory was six now. It was time for Big School.

Two days before the school opened, Mam's tiredness
passed.

'This can't go on,' she complained, leaping out of bed at
seven in the morning, 'this house needs cleaning.' She got her
mop and bucket, her brushes and her hoover, her polish and
her dusters and scrubbed and rubbed. Kitchen, living-room,

toilet and shower, bedrooms, kitchen presses, windows and doors shone and sparkled once again. The mug behind thebathroom curtains went into the bin.

She sat down exhausted from her work. Then she phoned Mr Dandelion and told him she'd like to start work if he still had a job for her.

'A good worker is always welcome,' he told her, 'drop round on Monday and you can start immediately.'

The big school was a red building just four doors away from the house. The morning it opened Rory screamed and bellowed. Mam had bought him an orange-coloured lunchbox and a red and green schoolbag.

He kicked the bag under the table and turned his lunchbox upside down on the kitchen floor. Then he flung his banana up in the air and stamped on his turkey sandwich.

'I don't want to go,' roared Rory, 'I'M NOT GOING.'

'Every child must go to school. You should have been at big school two years ago. My nerves are in bits from you.

YOU'RE GOING TO SCHOOL' insisted Mam, putting his bag on his back and dragging him out the door.

The noise was deafening all the way down the road. Her ears were ringing by the time they reached the school gate.

There were eighteen children starting that day, ten girls and eight boys.

Two little girls were crying because they'd never been to Big School before but Mrs Tilly Turnip was a nice kind teacher and she told them that it was a lovely place and that they'd make friends and play games and learn lots of wonderful things. Soon the little girls stopped sobbing and sat down in their seats.

All the children were sitting quietly at their desks when a loud kicking noise came from outside the classroom door.

'Dear, oh dear,' said Mrs Turnip, 'what can that noise be? Open the door, Jasmine Tomato, and see if there's a bear, a lion or even a stripy tiger in the corridor.'

Jasmine Tomato was a big child. She was a strong child.

She was a brave child. She jumped up and opened the door and then with a loud crash she fell back on her bottom.

'Goodness me, what's going on here?' said Mrs Turnip.

'Sorry, teacher, sorry little girl,' said Mam Rashers, 'he didn't mean to kick you. He was just kicking the door when you opened it.' Her cheeks were red with embarrassment.

'Well, well,' said Mrs Turnip, and she turned to Rory.

'What a big boy we have here. What age is this fine fellow?' she asked his Mam.

'Six, teacher. I kept him home because…because…because…'

'Well he should have more sense then. Most of the children in this class are just four. Sit down, boy,' she demanded, 'and I MEAN now! Say bye-bye to your Mam and sit beside Sean Sandwich. All right? Hop to.'

'Sean Sandwich, that's a stupid name,' Rory sniggered.
'I said sit down, and please mind your manners,' said the teacher.

Rory grabbed his Mam's skirt and almost pulled it off her.

'I'm not staying here,' he roared, 'I want to go home. WAH, WAH, WAH. Take me out of this horrible stinky place.'

'Stop pulling at your Mam, you naughty boy, ' ordered Mrs Turnip. 'Here, let me look at you.'

She put on her glasses and glared at him. Rory's Mam closed the classroom door. When he saw she'd gone, he roared again.

'Come back, Mam, come back. MAAAAAAAAM!'

'Stand up,' shouted Mrs Turnip, 'turn your face to the wall and don't open your mouth. And I mean that. DO YOU HEAR ME?'

Her round turnipy face got very cross and little bits of sweat rolled down her forehead. But Rory just kept on roaring.

'Outside the door this very minute,' said Mrs Turnip.
Rory had to stand there until the bell rang for lunch.

He'd been roaring so loud and for so long that his voice wouldn't come out any more. She called him back into the classroom and told him to sit beside Sean Sandwich.'

Sean Sandwich was a happy boy. A friendly boy. A generous boy.

'Here,' he said, offering some of his lunch to Rory, 'my Ma made me three banana sandwiches, two egg sandwiches and one tomato sandwich. Take your pick.'

Rory grabbed one of Sean's egg sandwiches and squashed it all over the desk.

'Yuk, yuk, yuk,' he said, 'keep your smelly old sandwiches, Yuk, Yuk, Yuk.'

While the children ate their lunch, Mrs Turnip sat knitting a purple and green jumper for her husband Sam. Last term she'd knitted him thick woollen socks and when she was finished the jumper she was going to knit him a warm orange vest. He was the captain of a big ship and he needed warm clothes when he sailed on the high seas around Alaska and other strange places. She was so busy watching her stitches she didn't see Rory squashing Sean's sandwich.

'Now children,' she said, putting away her knitting, 'get into your line and we'll go out to the yard.'

Rory was delighted the stupid old bag was so busy at her stitches she didn't spot him squashing the sambo.

Chapter 4

The Hole in the Bushes

When the children were all lined up, Mrs Turnip went round the desks picking up the leavings from their lunches. When she came to Sean and Rory's desk she saw the squashed egg sandwich. Her face turned black with temper.

'Who, may I ask, caused this mess?' she asked.

By this time Rory's voice had come back. 'I did,' he admitted, 'but it's none of your business, horse face. It was a horrible manky old egg sandwich anyway. If you ate it you'd probably die in five minutes.'

'How dare you,' said Mrs Turnip, 'God give me patience. You're a vulgar, nasty boy. I'll talk to you after break.' Her face got blacker and blacker with rage.

All the teachers went to the staff room for tea while the children played in the yard.

Dolly Apple Bee taught Senior Infants and was pouring herself a cup of tea when Mrs Turnip came in.

'What a morning,' sighed Mrs Turnip, 'I've a little demon in my class. I can see already he'll be trouble with a capital T.'

'I heard the screams of him in the corridor,' replied Dolly, 'sounds some boyo all right.'

Percy Boxer Shorts had his nose stuck in the newspaper as ususal.

Just then Maudie Umbrella Legs walked in.

'How do, all,' she chirped in her bright cheery way, 'enjoy the holliers?'

'Yes, but one day back here and it's like you were never away,' replied Mrs Turnip, 'I was just telling Dolly I've a right little tulip in my class.'

'I'm sure he'll settle down. Remember, don't smile till Christmas. That's the way to deal with them. Treat them mean, keep them keen,' advised Maudie with a laugh.

Percy raised his head from his paper. He was a small man with a balding head and a forehead that always frowned.

'As far as I'm concerned, don't smile at them at all or the little ruffians will drive you nuts. I had a fine head of hair three years ago. A fine head of hair. Look at the state of me now.'

'Ah well, look on the bright side - only three months to Christmas,' consoled Maudie as she munched into a large chocolate éclair.

'I'm definitely on a diet from tomorrow,' she promised. 'My spare tyre is only massive.'

'Tomorrow and tomorrow and tomorrow,' snorted Percy, 'why does nobody ever start a diet today?'

'Get stuffed,' said Maudie, licking large blobs of chocolate and cream from her thumb.

The school yard was large, with a green patch to play football and a stony place to skip or play hide-and-seek. The girls and boys ran round like leaves blowing in the September wind. Some girls played skipping and the boys kicked football like mad. Nobody played with Rory because if a child came near him he kicked them in the ankle or pinched them on the bottom.

'This place makes me sick, ' he said to himself.

He wandered away from the other children towards some bushes at the corner of the schoolyard. A girl was sitting on a low wall. He noticed she was crying.

'What are you crying for, silly girl?' he asked. The girl didn't answer him, she just kept on crying her huge tears.

'Are you deaf? ' screamed Rory poking the little girl in the tummy, 'what's wrong with you? Stop that sniffling.'

'I can't skip,' whispered the little girl, whose name was Katie Carrots.

'Can't skip? That's funny.' He threw back his head and screamed with laughter. 'Silly old cry baby, go home to your Mammy and she'll dry up your tears for you.'

Walking away he noticed a hole in the thick dark bushes. He bent down to see where it would lead. Crawling through the hole he pushed his way through brambles and thorns.

His face and legs were scratched but he kept on going.

He didn't hear the school bell ring and he didn'tsee that all the children were back in their classrooms.

Suddenly he heard a loud voice. 'Oh,' he said, 'what's that horrible noise?'

'It's me. My tough old boots are pinching me. I've a pain in my back and I hate this boring schoolyard with it's boring, boring children.'

Rory stared all round but could see nothing. Then he looked down and there was the smallest man he'd ever seen. He was wearing purple trousers, a bright red jacket, a pointed yellow cap and his toes were poking out of his little brown boots. 'Go away, you dirty little thing,' roared Rory, 'buzz off with yourself.'
'Don't you dare talk to me like that. If I were your dad I'd take the stick to you, you bad mannered youngster,' said the little man crossly.

'Well you're not my dad,' said Rory. 'My dad is big and strong and has eyes like the sea.'

'Give me a break,' said the little man. 'Eyes like the sea. Probably looks like a smelly old fish.'

'Shut your trap.'

'I'll sort you out,' rasped the little man as he waved his small fist at Rory.

'Who's going to sort me out - you and whose army?' yelled Rory. He reached down and lifted the man up in the air and plonked him down on the palm of his hand.

'Put me down, you cruel boy', the man screamed, stamping his little feet up and down on Rory's hand.
'Stop screaming,' Rory told him, 'I've a pain in me head

from you. Have a bit of manners.' He caught the little man's nose and twisted it round and round between his fingers.

'I'll soon put manners on you, shorty,' he sniggered.

The little man continued bawling until Rory was almost deaf. He opened his mouth as wide as he could to roar

back at him, and when he did the man leapt from his hand, hopped into his mouth, flew straight down his throat and into his tummy.

'Mam, Mam, ' screamed Rory, 'HELP!'

The screams from his stomach got louder and Rory pushed his way back out of the hole and raced back into the yard.

Chapter 5

Mam Forgets One Of Her Shoes

Mrs Turnip and Mrs Jam, the head teacher, were in the schoolyard calling his name.

'There you are, you rascal,' said Mrs Jam. 'Mrs Turnip has been very upset about you, my fine fellow. You've disrupted her class and called her a rude name.

In this school, when the bell rings you go to your line like all the other children. Do you hear that, disobedient boy?'

'Missus, missus, help me,' said Rory, 'there's a little man in me stomach.' 'I'll give you a man in your stomach if you're not careful. And it's MY stomach. ME is incorrect,' said Mrs Jam. Then she snarled, 'Come to my office this very instant. I'm going to phone your mother and tell her about your carry-on. As I'm sick telling you, we do NOT keep bold boys in our school.'

'Please, missus, do you not hear him? He's screaming. Put your ear down and you will. Please missus, I'm scared.'

Mrs Jam took Rory's arm and dragged him down a long corridor and into her dusty office.

'Sit there,' she hissed. 'Two girls and one boy had to get plasters on their legs because you kicked them. I don't want to hear another peep from you. Not another peep.'

She picked up the phone and rang Rory's Mam.

Rory sat listening to the loud screams. He rubbed his tummy thinking it might quieten the horrible little man. But he kept on screaming.

'Missus, Missus, come here. Listen to it,' Rory demanded after she hung up the phone.

After a few minutes Mam came running down the corridor. Her red hair was sticking out and she'd forgotten to put on one of her shoes.

'Now, Mam Rashers,' said Mrs Jam, 'I'm sorry to tell you your son has been very very naughty and you must take him home this instant because I can't hear myself think. When he's ready to be a good boy we'll take him back into our school.' Then she added firmly, 'But I can't see that happening.'

'I'm sorry, teacher,' said Rory's Mam, 'he does roar a lot but he doesn't mean it.'

'There's more to it,' said Mrs Jam, banging her hand on the desk, 'He kicked four children in the playground and squashed Sean Sandwich's egg sandwich on our good desk. He was extremely rude to his teacher. He hid in the bushes when break was over. And he never ever stops roaring.'

'He'll be a good boy from now on, won't you Rory?' pleaded Mam.

'Mam, Mam, will you listen to the little man,.' said Rory, 'He's in me tummy. I mean MY tummy. Mam I'm afraid. WAH WAH WAH WAH.'

'Now, now, Rory, be quiet. I promise you, Mrs Jam, he'll be a good boy if you give him one more chance.'

'Take the boy home NOW,' Mrs Jam ordered, 'my head is only splitting. IF, and it's a big IF, if he promises to be good and stops that awful roaring we may take him back next week.'

Mam grabbed Rory by the hand and walked grimly out the gate. All the way home Rory could still hear the shouting in his belly as Mam's grip tightened on him.

Chapter 6

No Sleep for Rory

When they got home, Rory ran upstairs. He stood in front of the bathroom mirror and opened his mouth to see if he could see the little man.

But all that was there was his own pink tongue waggling back at him. 'Mam,' he panted, running down the stairs, 'turn down the telly. Please Mam, will you? LISTEN.'

'Rory, I'm tired listening to you. 'I've just got my job back. Mr Dandelion has very kindly taken me backand I'm to start tomorrow. If you don't stop your tricks I'll have to stay at home again. I don't want to do that, much as I love you. You have to go to school like every other child in the world.'

'Mam, will you just listen to my stomach? You have to, have to, have to.' 'What are talking about? What's wrong with your stomach? Have you a pain?'

'No, Mam, not a pain. A man flew in, Mam. Can you not hear him?'

'A man flew in. I suppose you'll be telling me it was the man in the moon next. I don't want any more fairytales from you, sir. I'm too tired after my day's work. I just want to have a cup of coffee and some crisps and get forty winks.'

Rory was always making up stories. Mam remembered the day he told her a man from Mars was at the front door with a green head and two big ears sticking out of the top of it. Imagine that. A man from Mars who had a tin bucket and wanted Mam to buy a raffle ticket for the new ward at the hospital.

'Pull the other one,' Mam had told Rory that day, 'it's got bells on.' Rory didn't know what that meant but he knew his trick hadn't worked. Mars was too far away for Mam to believe him, and people with green ears were only in films or on the telly on Saturday morning in the children's programmes.

'THAT'S why she won't believe me,' Rory told himself, almost close to tears. Mam looked to be in pain.

'But Mam, I'm telling you. I went into the bushes and he flew in. He has purple trousers and his boots are hurting him. Mam, I saw him. Listen. Can you not hear the scary noises he's making?'

Mam put her ear down to please him even though she didn't believe a word of it. 'I don't hear anything. Now go up to your room. I want to watch the telly. You have my heart scalded with your antics.'

Rory sat on the stairs listening to the loud noise. Suddenly the screaming stopped and he could hear the man talking to himself.

'I'm sick of this fellow's stomach,' said the voice, 'he broke my poor nose, and now I've landed myself in this dark gooey place. HELP, HELP, LET ME OUT.'

'Stop it!' demanded Rory, 'will you leave me alone and get out of there, you dirty rotten thing you.' But the little man didn't seem to hear. He just continued muttering to himself.

The little man's voice started up again: 'Why wouldn't that ignorant lump of boy have a nice dinner of bacon and cabbage or maybe fish fingers and beans instead of drowning me with fizzy drinks and poisoning me with rubbishy sweets?'

Rory climbed the stairs and went into the bathroom. He washed his teeth and got into his blue pyjamas. He lay down on his bed but couldn't sleep because of the noise.

After a long time he heard Mam come up the stairs to bed and he called out to her.

'Mam, please, will you come here?'

'Go to sleep. This is getting beyond a joke.'

'Mam, I'm frightened, he won't stop talking. The noise,
Mam, it's so LOUD.'

But Mam went into her bedroom and soon he could
hear her snores.
Rory sat up in his bed with his hands pressed against his ears.

'Maybe if I stand on my head he'll fly out my mouth,' he said
to himself. So for five minutes he did that until he felt the
blood flooding into him like thunder.

It was all for nothing. The awful noise went on, on, on,
like a broken record.

Suddenly after a long time everything was quiet for a
few seconds. But then Rory felt as if his tummy was
being kicked like a football.

'How do you like them onions, Rashers,' screamed the
little man.

'Go away you. Please please go away. You're hurting me.'

But the little man continued to kick.

Poor Rory sat on his bed for hours and hours and hours.
After a long time he saw the sky getting salmony pink
and he heard the birds singing and the postman and
milkman doing their rounds and other children laughing
on their way to school. He'd been awake the whole long night.

Chapter 7

Plum Tart for Conor and Pink Toenails for Mam

Rory opened his window wide and leaned his head out.
It was a beautiful morning. He saw old Mr Cheese next
door weeding his garden.

'Morning to you, Rory my lad,' called Mr Cheese. But
Rory couldn't hear him because of the noise.
I said GOOD MORNING RORY,' Mr Cheese repeated.

'What did you say? I can't hear you.'

'MORNING!' screamed Mr Cheese.

'Morning, Mr Cheese,' said Rory in a small voice.

'It's good to hear you talking like everybody else,' called
Mr Cheese, 'it makes a nice change from all your roaring.
My grandson Conor is coming over today. He's a bit older
than you but maybe you could play a game of football
with him.' Then Mr Cheese went into his house to have
his boiled egg and toast with Mrs Cheese.

'That young fellow Rory next door is getting manners at
last,' he told Mrs Cheese. 'He was as polite as can be and
didn't even call me cheeseburger like he usually does.'

'I should hope so,' said his wife, 'I still wouldn't him
let him near our Conor, though. He has no manners. I
feel sorry for his poor mother. She has her hands full
with him. I was thinking of making a plum tart for Conor.
He just loves plum tart.'

'Wouldn't say no to a slice myself,' Mr Cheese chortled,
'nobody makes plum tart like you do, sweetie. It's nice
and soft and I don't have to use those awful new teeth of
mine. 300 euro I paid for a load of rubbish.'

Mam was eating her cornflakes when he came
downstairs. She had curlers in her hair and she was
wearing her old worn-out dressing-gown.

'You don't deserve a breakfast,' she rasped, 'I should be on
the bus with the other women going to work. And you,
my fine fellow, should be at school. Mary Rose and myself
were supposed to be going into town on Saturday and now
I can't go because I have no money.

You really are a handful, Rory Rashers, a right handful.'

'I don't want any breakfast, Mam. He's still in there.'
'What are you on about, Rory? Who's in there?'

'The man, Mam, I told you. He's in me stomach.
When he stops shouting he starts to kick me.'

'If I hear that again I'll go mad. There's nothing in
your stomach. Sit down there. I'll make you some toast
and you'll be right as rain in no time.'

'I don't want toast. Can you not hear him, Mam? I'm deaf
from it. He never stopped all night.'

'Rory, will you stop that carry-on. Sit up there at the
table and eat your breakfast.'

'Mam, just put your ear down. Please Mam, will you?
Go on Mam. PLEASE.'

Mam bent down and and put her ear to his belly. She
could hear nothing only a little gurgle of hunger.

'That's your tummy. We all have that. It's wind. Eat
up your breakfast and it'll go away.'

'But the talking. It's so loud. Please Mam. Bring me to
the doctor. Please, Mam, will you?'

'You don't need a doctor, except may be a doctor for the
head. I'll need one if you don't stop talking about men in
your stomach. There's no noise, Rory. No noise.'

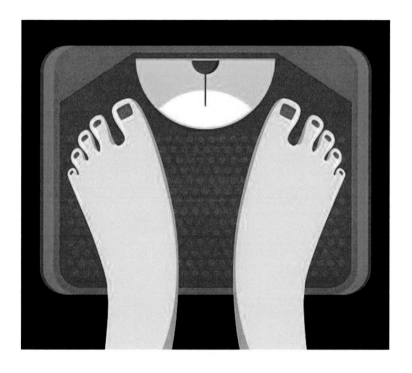

She buttered her toast and after she'd eaten it she got her bottle of dusky pink nail polish and started painting her dainty little toenails.

Chapter 8

Rory Behaves Himself

Rory went back to his bedroom and lay on his bed crying. CHATTER, CHATTER, CHATTER went his tummy. KICK, KICK, KICK went the tiny feet.

He fell asleep after a little while and dreamed that the little man had been joined by his whole family. There were two boys even smaller than the man, and a girl wearing a bright red cardigan. They were all wearing big hobnailed boots and were dancing round and round inside his poor tummy.

'Wake up Rory, we're going to the shops,' announced his Mam as she shook him.

When he opened his eyes, Rory thought the whole thing was a big long dream. But then he heard the noise again and he knew it wasn't.

'Mam it's still there,' he groaned.

'I can't hear you, Rory. What's the matter with your voice? Speak up.'

'The man. He's still there.'

'Not again, Rory. God give me strength. Go and clean your face and help me get the shopping.'

In the supermarket Rory was quiet. He picked up the tins of beans and the cornflakes packet and the tea bags and never once asked his Mam for sweets.

'You're being very good, Rory,' a surprised Mama remarked. 'If this continues maybe we'll ask the teachers to take you back tomorrow.'

'Great!'

On the way home from the shops they met Sean Sandwich.

'Hi, Rory. Are you coming to school tomorrow?'

Rory could barely hear Sean's voice.

'I don't know. By the way, sorry about messing up your egg sambo.'

'No probs,' said Sean. 'See you tomorrow.'

'We'll call into see Mrs Turnip now,' said Mam, 'and if you say you're very sorry maybe she'll take you back.'

Mrs Turnip was closing the classroom door when they arrived at the school.

'Now, Rory,' said Mam, 'What do you say to teacher?'

'I'm sorry,' mumbled Rory.

'I beg your pardon,' said Mrs Turnip, putting her hand to her ear, 'Speak up, lad.'

'I'm sorry.'

'Well maybe we'll give you another chance,' grunted Mrs Turnip. 'You can come to school tomorrow. But remember - NO ROARING. I'm glad to see you're quiet now. Keep that up and you can stay.'

'Thank you, teacher,' said Rory softly. Mam took his hand and he walked home with her with a pep in his step.

Chapter 9

Back to the Hole in the Bushes

That night Rory didn't sleep again. All night long the loud noise and kicking kept going on and on and on.

When morning came he slowly made his way downstairs. He was exhausted. Mam was setting the table with her coat on.

'Hurry up, Rory,' she pressed. 'Eat your breakfast quickly or I'll miss the bus to work.'

'Yes, Mam.'

He gobbled up his breakfast and they left the house together. When they got to the school he waved politely to Mam and went inside. He sat down at his desk and kept very very quiet. He didn't pinch or push anybody or pull any little girl's hair.

At lunchtime he shared his bar of chocolate with Sean Sandwich and gave Mary Marzipan a bit of his orange.

It was a lovely sunny day and all the children ran around playing. Rory sat quietly by himself listening to the terrible noise inside him.

A little girl call Sarah Salad fell and cut her knee. Rory raced over to her, helped her up and brought her to Mrs Turnip.

'Don't cry, Sarah,' consoled Rory, 'it's only a little cut.'

'Thank you, Rory' Mrs Turnip beamed, 'I'm proud of you.'

Wiping her tears away, Sarah asked Rory to sit beside her after the break.

He wandered over towards the hole in the hedge where he'd first seen the little man. Katie, the little girl who couldn't skip, was sitting on the wall looking very lonely.

'Don't be sad,' Rory told her, 'you'll soon learn.'

'Thanks,' said Katie, 'maybe I will.'

'Why are you always on your own?' asked Rory. 'If you go over to the girls you'll learn to skip.'

'But I'm sad,' explained Katie. And then she whispered, 'My dad's gone away.'

'Mine too, said Rory, but I've got a lovely Mam.'

'Mine's lovely too,' Katie grinned.

And she walked towards the skipping girls.

Rory bent his head and peeped into the hole. He crawled through the bushes.

'Home at last,' said the voice from his stomach. 'Yippee, Yippee, home at last.'

'Open that mouth of yours, boy. Give a big cough and for goodness sake let me out of here.'

'What did you say?'

'What's your problem? Are you deaf? Open your mouth, give a big cough and let me out of this awful place,' screamed the little man.

Rory opened his mouth and coughed and coughed as hard as he could until his face turned bright purple. Suddenly the little man flew out with a big WHOOSH and raced away into the dark bushes.

'Peace, peace, beautiful peace,' he screamed as he ran away. Rory felt the way you do when you burp, or when a big lump of ice-cream that you ate too quick and stuck in your stomach suddenly seems to disappear.

Far away he heard the school bell ringing. He was so happy he could hardly breathe. Now it didn't matter if anyone believed him or not. He was free. Both of them were free.

He scrambled out of the hole and raced down to join the other children. He could hear the noise their shoes made on the stone schoolyard and it was like music to his ears. Not one sound came from his tummy.

'Very good work, Rory,' said Mrs Turnip as she checked his colouring later on that day, 'Are you sure you're the same boy who was here two days ago?' Rory had no answer to that.

Chapter 10

A Letter from Cavan

The months passed by. Rory went to school every day and no longer roared or screamed. Mam continued to work in the crisp factory and she didn't look tired or sad anymore.

Rory and Sean Sandwich became great friends and they often slept over in each other's houses.

One morning three weeks before Christmas a letter came, addressed to Mam. They were just getting ready to leave the house but she sat down on the doorstep to read it.

Her pink cheeks turned pale and the letter fell from her hand.

'What is it, Mam?' quizzed Rory. 'Who's the letter from?'

'It's from your dad,' she answered in a weak wobbly voice. 'Where is he? Read it to me.'

'Come back into the house, Rory, love. We're going to take the day off. 'I'll make a call to Mr Dandelion. He won't mind for one day, and you can take a break from school.'

'But it's art today, and I love art.'

'We need to talk. This is important, Rory.'

They went back into the house. Mam put on the kettle for tea. Rory took out their two blue mugs and when the kettle boiled they sat down at the table. Mam started to speak. 'He lives in Cavan. He has a partner called Phyllis and twin girls aged three. He says he wants to meet you.'

'Cavan? Where's that? And twin girls - why not boys?

I hate dirty old Phyllis. I hate twin girls. I hate my dad. Why didn't he write before?'

'I don't know. I'm weak with shock'

 'Well he can hump off with himself,' snarled Rory, 'he should have written before.'

'That doesn't matter. He's writing *now*. Those little girls are your half-sisters, Rory.'

'I don't want half-sisters. I don't even want full sisters. I don't want to go to Cavan. I don't want to see him.'

They sat at the table until the winter evening crept
into the hall, into the dusty corners of the kitchen and
upstairs into the dark quiet bedrooms.

'Right,' said Mam. 'He's your dad, Rory. The decision
is made. On Saturday we get the bus to Cavan.'

'But Mam, I told you, I don't want to go. I hate Cavan.
It's a rotten old place.'

'Saturday we go to Cavan,' insisted Mam, 'and that's
my final word.'

Chapter 11

Going Fishing

On Saturday morning Mam and Rory were on the bus to Cavan. Neither of them talked very much as the bus sped along.

After a long silence Rory spoke.

'What's Cavan like? Is it a big place?'

'Probably not. All I know is the towns. Cavan, Cootehill and Belturbet. How's that for a memory. Learnt that when I was ten years old, so I did.'

'Cavan, Cootehill and Belturnip. Stupid names, just like Mrs Turnip. It must be a yucky place.'

'Belturbet, *not* Belturnip, Rory,'

'Last Stop Cavan,' called the driver, 'all passengers must disembark here.'

Rory held Mam's hand as they walked away from the bus.

The streets were deserted except for a fat woman pushing an old-fashioned shopping trolley. A grey drizzly rain was blowing in the wind.

'Dirty old day,' she grumbled as she passed them by.
'Oh,' said Mam, 'Look, Rory, there he is.'

A tall man with black hair came towards them.

He was dressed in football gear. He kicked a ball towards
Rory.

Rory was delighted. He kicked it back.

'Maybe we could go for a bite to eat,' suggested the
man, 'There's a lovely café just across the road.'

They followed him into a warm, jolly-looking restaurant.

There were striped cloths on the table and a delicious
smell of baking coming from the kitchen.

'Sit yourself down,' said the man,' and order whatever
you want.

They have apple tart, cream buns, ice cream, and the most
delicious chocolate cake you ever heard of. The twins adore it.
Pick what you want.'

'I'll have a cup of tea,' said Mam, 'Rory, you might like the
chocolate cake. That's your favourite.'

Rory said he wasn't hungry and wanted to go home.

Mam barely sipped at her tea. Rory stared out the window at
the driving rain.

'Would you like to come back to the house and meet Phyllis
and the girls?' suggested the man after a long silence.

'I want to go home,' grunted Rory, 'me and Mam want to go
back to our own house.'

'Now, Rory, don't be rude. Your dad just wants to
show you his house and his little girls. Go with him.
I'll sit here and drink my tea.'

Rory opened his mouth to roar, but then remembered
the little man in the bushes. Instead he stayed quiet.

'Come on,' said the man, 'I'll drive you back to the house.
You can meet the girls. I'll have you back to your Mam in
an hour, just in time for the evening bus.'

'Go on,' Mam repeated, 'there's a good boy. I'll be here
waiting for you when you get back.' She gave him a little
smile.

Rory followed the man out of the café. Mam picked up
the menu but didn't order anything.

She just sat in the empty café, stirring and stirring her cold tea.
The man's car was big and looked new and shiny. Rory sat in
the back seat gazing out the window until they got to the
house.

It was white with a dark red door and a huge garden. It
wasn't like the Dublin house. It stood alone in a field
and there were no other houses to be seen anywhere.

The door burst open as the car pulled in to the driveway.
Two plump little girls rushed out.
'Daddy, daddy,' they called and threw themselves into
the man's open arms.

A tall thin woman stood in the hallway. She had yellow
hair, not as nice as Mam's, and lots of red lipstick.

'Hello, Rory,' she said. 'Come in. You're welcome, my dear.'
The twins were exactly the same. Rory couldn't work
out which was Bess and which was Tess. They both
had pigtails tied with red ribbons and both of their
button noses were covered in freckles.

They pulled at Rory, pleading with him to come and
see their play-room.

'Rory and I want to have a chat,' said the man. 'Leave
him alone, girls. Come on, Rory, son, we'll go and sit
at the nice fire.'
Rory followed him into a cosy sitting-room.

'A fire,' said an excited Rory, 'a REAL fire.'

'That's right son, a real fire. I bet you don't have real fires
in Dublin.'

'We've radiators, one in every room.'

'Well you can't beat a turf fire. Maybe if you come up
to me in the summer I'll bring you to the bog for a day
and we can cut turf together.'

'I don't want to cut turf. Why did you leave my Mam? There
was a long silence. 'You're far too young to be asking
questions like that,'said the man.

There was another long silence except for the fire
crackling.

After a while the man sighed and sat down beside Rory.

He talked and Rory listened. He told Rory he loved
him. He said he cried every night for six weeks after he
left Mam. He would never forgive himself for that as
long as he lived. Could Rory forgive him?

'I want to go back to Mam,' was all Rory said. The man
talked for a long time more but Rory didn't understand
what he was saying. Then he was silent again, staring into
the dying embers.

'I want to go back to Mam,' Rory demanded.

'Ok sonny, back we'll go,' said the man. 'Won't you say
goodbye to your little sisters.'

'They're not my sisters. I have no sisters.'

Rory sat back into the car. Phyllis and the little girls
stood waving at the door but he never looked at them.

When they reached the town he rushed out of the car,
chased into the café, and flung himself into Mam's
comforting arms. The man walked them to the bus.

'I'll keep in touch, Bridget,' he promised, 'you've done a
great
job on Rory. He's a fine boy. You should be proud of him.'

'He's the best,' Mam agreed, 'the very best.'

In the springtime the man came to visit them. He took
Rory and Mam to an adventure film and afterwards they had
chips and burgers in MacDonalds. Rory told Mam it was an
OK night.

When summer came, Rory went to stay for the weekend with
the man, the twins and Phyllis.

Rory now decided Cavan wasn't too bad after all. The twins
were very funny. Phyllis read a story and the man played
football in the field behind the house with Rory. Next summer
he's going to bring him fishing.

Mam still works in the crisp factory. Mr Dandelion has asked
her to accompany him to the New Year's Ball. She looks
happier.

Sometimes when Rory is in bed he can hear her singing.

Chapter 12

One Year Later

Conor Cheese is twelve now. He's broken every window in
his grandparent's house. They don't want him to visit
anymore.

Mrs Toffee closed the playschool and opened a fish
and chip shop. The chips are chunky and gorgeous.

Covid had arrived so they all had to wear masks.

The serious lady who did the lunches took up running. She's training for the next Olympics. She's a very good runner. She may win a gold medal.

Katie's Mam and Dad are back together. Katie skips all the way to bed every night with delight.

Jack Toenails is a genius. He's going to university next September. He was only seven on his last birthday.

Mrs Turnip's husband is home from his travels. Every evening at half past seven they go for a stroll together.

Dolly Apple Bee is getting married in June.

Maudie Umberella is going on a diet. *Tomorrow.*

Percy Boxer Shorts has bought himself a wig. It's black, coal black.

Mrs Jam moved to a school down the country. The children are far better behaved there.

The fat lady in Cavan won a car in the Lotto. She doesn't have to pull her trolley anymore.

The boy with the black spiky hair and his skinny mother went to Australia. He took up surfing and is loving it. She became a model and is on the telly over there.

Mary Rose met a soldier. They're going to Greece together in April.

Carol has opened two more *Carol's Cut and Curl Up* salons. One is in the Northside Shopping Centre and the other is in Kilbarrack. They're both going a bomb.

Mrs Bathtub's leg still pains her. She uses a stick now.

Phyllis, the man and the twins are moving to Dublin.

Rory and his Mam are checking out suitable places for them just off the Artane roundabout.

The little man in the bushes is still in there. Last week he bought a new pair of boots. They pinch too.

Daisy Pinks is hoping to be a bridesmaid soon. Her brother is in love with a woman in the factory. She's lovely. Her name is Bridget Rashers. She has a son. Not a bad little chap. His name is Rory. Daisy is keeping her fingers crossed - and her toes.

It would be nice to have a sister-in-law. Every night she dreams it will happen. Maybe someday her dream will come true.

Just before Christmas Mam painted the white zig-zag waves and the golden stars. Rory painted in the big fat yellow moon.

THE END